WARREN
& Dragon

100 Friends

WARREN &Dragon

100
Friends

by Ariel Bernstein

Illustrated by Mike Malbrough

VIKING

VIKING

Penguin Young Readers
An imprint of Penguin Random House LLC
375 Hudson Street
New York, New York 10014

First published in the United States of America by Viking,
an imprint of Penguin Random House LLC, 2018

Text copyright © 2018 by Ariel Bernstein
Illustrations copyright © 2018 by Mike Malbrough

LIBRARY OF CONGRESS CATALOGING-IN-PUBLICATION DATA IS AVAILABLE
ISBN 9780425288443

Printed in U.S.A.

1   3   5   7   9   10   8   6   4   2

✖ ✖ ✖

For Scott, my best friend —A.B.

To my best bud, Abe —M.M.

✖ ✖ ✖

CONTENTS

1
Time to Pack

2
How to Make Friends

3
The Friend That Doesn't Count

4
Pie Contest

1

Time to Pack

"Warren Reginald Nesbitt! Are you even listening to us?" my mom says with her hands on her hips. My dad is standing next to her with his hands on his hips, too. They look like twins, which is funny because I really am a seven-year-old twin with my sister, Ellie.

"Yes," I say, wondering what I missed. I was watching Dragon, my pet dragon, slide down a banister in the living room onto a speeding skateboard.

"Have you started to pack?" Mom asks.

"I've packed lots," I say. I do not say I have not packed anything.

"What are we packing for?" Dragon whispers to me. I shrug because I don't know. "Are we going camping?" Dragon asks.

Dragon loves camping because of the roasted marshmallows.

"What do I have to pack exactly?" I ask my parents.

My parents' mouths drop open at the same time.

"Your toys, Warren," Mom says slowly. "Every toy you want to take when we move to the new house in Eddington. It's the only thing we've asked you to do."

"We're moving?!" Dragon says. He doesn't like change. "Quick, pack all the marshmallows!"

My parents don't notice Dragon running into the kitchen to find the marshmallows. No one notices anything Dragon does except me, but I like it that way.

"When are we moving?" I ask. Their mouths drop open again.

"Next Friday, right before Labor Day weekend," Mom says, and shakes her head. She shakes her head a lot when she talks to me.

"We've talked about it for five months now," Dad says.

I try to remember the past five months. One day Dragon and I made a fort out of bedsheets and chairs in my bedroom and Dad came in.

"If you ruin those sheets or chairs I'm not buying new ones for the next house," he said.

Another day Dragon and I made a snack of marshmallows, blueberries, and peanut butter in the juicer and forgot to put the lid on. When Mom saw the kitchen she said, "Do I need to clean if we're moving in two months?"

Then there was the day Dragon and I jumped up and down on a bunch of boxes in Ellie's room. She got upset and told Mom we ruined all of her perfect packing. Mom told me to spend my energies packing and not jumping.

"I might remember something about this," I say just as Ellie walks into the room.

Even though we're twins, Ellie and I don't look much alike. Ellie looks like our dad with their blond hair, brown eyes, and freckles on their noses. I look like Mom with our brown hair, green eyes, and freckles on our arms. Dragon doesn't look like anybody, because he's a dragon.

"He's never going to pack in time," Ellie says. "If Warren doesn't pack all his toys by moving day, can we stay?"

"No. We are moving, Ellie," Mom says.

"You don't want to move?" I ask.

"Why would I want to move?" Ellie asks as though I'm supposed to know the answer. I do not know the answer. "I have *all* my friends here and my basketball team and my gymnastics class. Why did you have to get a new job in a new town, Mom?"

"We've been over this, Ellie. I had to find a new job when the company I worked for closed," Mom tells her. "And I was lucky to find another engineer position so quickly."

"Honey, you'll make new friends when you start second grade and join new activities," Dad adds.

"I'll still miss my friends here."

"I won't," I say. "Your friends smell like rotten pumpkins."

"*Mom!*" Ellie shouts, and crosses her arms.

"Okay, okay. They don't all smell like rotten pumpkins," I say.

"Hmph," Ellie says.

"Some of them smell like rotten pickles."

"*Mom!*"

"I'm just trying to help you so you won't miss everybody," I say. I do not say I'm not really trying to help.

"Don't you two remember you used to get along?" Mom asks. "I have a photo somewhere of you playing in the sand together. Maybe it's in the photo albums I packed. I'll have to unpack it...."

"Don't unpack!" Dad says. "No . . . one . . . unpack . . . anything!"

"I don't mind moving," I say. And it's true. I won't have to listen to our neighbor Ms. Reilly call me "Warri-Boo" anymore.

"That's because you don't have any friends," Ellie says.

"That's not true!" I do not say it might be true. "Dragon is my friend."

"Dragon isn't real."

"I am so offended," Dragon says in between bites of marshmallow.

Ellie shakes her head. She looks a lot like Mom when she does that.

"You shouldn't offend Dragon. He gets scary when he's offended."

Dragon huffs and puffs as best he can.

"I don't care if he's real or not. You still get to bring him with us. I have to make all new friends."

"I have to make new friends at school, too."

"Really? *You're* going to make new friends?"

"Yeah, and I'm going to make more new friends than you," I say. I do not say I might not believe what I just said. I never made a friend before. I didn't have to because I've always had Dragon. But if Ellie can make friends, how hard can it be?

"Yes! Friends with marshmallows!" Dragon adds. "Warren, only make friends with kids who have marshmallows."

"*Ha!*" Ellie says. "There's no way you're going to make more friends than me!"

"I'm going to make a hundred new friends!" I tell her. I do not know why I keep talking.

"*Ha!*"

"Enough!" Dad says. "Warren, it's time."

"To make new friends?"

"To pack!"

2

How to Make Friends

"Ugh. How am I going to pack all this in one week?" I say, looking at my room.

"Don't pack everything," Dragon says. "Just the good stuff. Like me."

I lift up a plastic green tarantula and a blob of gooey fake ghost slime and toss them into a box.

"Everything I have is good."

"What about this?" Dragon asks, holding up the broken half of a blue crayon.

"I might need half of a blue crayon one day." I throw the crayon in the box and it splits into two more halves.

"Dragon, I need to make more friends than Ellie when we move."

"Why do you want to make more friends? You have me," Dragon says.

"Ellie's always right about everything," I say, and Dragon nods his head because he knows what I'm talking about. Ellie was right when she said the tub would flood if I put too many ninja toys near the drain, even though they really needed water training. She was right when she said my stomach would hurt from eating so many marshmallows at once, even though it was Dragon's idea to challenge me and he won anyway. And Ellie was right when she said if I didn't put on enough sunblock I'd get red, even though it was more important to help Dragon prepare for his annual fire-breathing exam that day. Dragon and I both ended up getting burned.

"I want to be right just one time," I say. "So how do I make friends?"

"That's easy," Dragon says. "When I want to make a new friend, I tell them they can either be my friend or I'll burn down their village."

"Dad says we're moving to a new town, not a village."

"Oh, that's a shame."

I find a smushed chocolate chip cookie under a pile of books. I break it in two and give half to Dragon.

"Still fresh," he says.

"I think it's only from a couple of months ago," I say.

"You know, people like compliments," Dragon says after licking the melted chocolate off his claws. "You can make friends fast by giving out compliments. Try it on me."

"Okay. You're very . . . dragon-y."

"That's not a compliment."

"You're slimy?"

"Also not a compliment. Compliments are supposed to make a friend feel good."

"Um . . . you smell especially smoky today."

"A little better. And?"

"Your tail is super spiky and a nice shade of green."

"It's not *just* green. It's emerald green!"

"Oh. Really?"

"Hmm . . . forget the compliments. Let's think of something else."

I pick up three monsters glued together. "I don't play with these anymore."

"They're my bodyguards," Dragon says.

"What do you need bodyguards for?"

"I'm very desirable."

"Okay," I say, and put the monsters into the box. "Hey! How did *we* become such good friends?"

"We have lots in common," Dragon says. "We both love marshmallows. We enjoy seeing how fast things can go down staircases. We like training worms to be ninja warriors. We're really good at getting out of bath time. And we both love marshmallows."

"So all I need is to find a hundred kids who love all the same stuff as me."

"Yes."

"I'm never going to make any friends," I say.

That night I dream about living in the new town. I show all the kids at school a magic show where I stuff my books into my backpack and then pull out a flying robot rabbit. Everybody wants to be my friend, but I only agree to be friends with the first hundred of them. Ellie sulks because no one wants to be her friend.

All of my friends want to sit next to me in class. At lunch my friends give me marshmallows so I'll eat next to them. At recess my friends play whatever I want. When I come home I hang out with Dragon, but Mom calls me to the front door. My one hundred friends are waiting to play with me.

"Leave me alone! I need a break!" I yell. All one hundred friends run away.

"I told you you'd never be able to make friends," Ellie says with a smirk.

I wake up next to a snoring Dragon.

"I'll show her," I say out loud. "I will make friends this time."

3

The Friend That Doesn't Count

I surprise everyone when I have my toys packed in time for moving day. It helped that Dragon and I pounded all my toys into the boxes so they'd fit.

The moving men put all the boxes into a huge truck, and Mom says we'll meet them at our new house later that day.

Everyone's quiet in the car. Too quiet.

"Are we there yet?" Dragon asks.

I don't think we are, but I ask anyway. "Are we there yet?"

"No," Dad says. "Don't ask that again."

"You ask," I whisper to Ellie. She giggles.

"Are we there yet?" she asks.

"I said not to ask that again!"

"Ellie asked, not me!"

"Don't start," Dad says.

"Are we there yet?" Dragon asks. "I'm hungry, and I've eaten all the marshmallows."

"So . . . am I there yet?" I say.

"Warren!"

"I didn't say 'we'!"

"Yeah, is Warren there yet?" Ellie asks.

"Yes, you can both get out," Dad grumbles.

"Dad said to get out!" I shout.

"You said it, Dad!" Ellie whoops.

"Look, Bill. They're getting along," Mom says as she pulls out her phone.

"Nora!" Dad says.

"I just want to get a photo real quick of them laughing together."

Dragon accidentally sits too close to Ellie and she throws him back at me.

"Hey, careful!" I say and point my finger at her.

"Mom! Warren's pointing his finger at me."

I point my finger closer. "I'm not touching you."

Ellie points her finger at Dragon. "I'm not touching Dragon," she says.

"Hey! Leave him alone!" I say.

"That tickles," Dragon says, giggling.

"No, wait!" Mom says. "You were just getting along. I almost had a photo of you both laughing."

"Everybody can get out," Dad mutters.

※　※　※

I think Dad is the happiest of us when we finally arrive at our new house in Eddington. I've seen photos of it online, but it looks smaller in person.

There's a bunch of people at the house next door looking at us from their porch. They walk over after Dad parks and we get out of the car.

"You must be our new neighbors," the taller of the two women says with a big smile. She's almost as tall as my dad. "Welcome to the neighborhood! I'm Paula Berry and this is my wife, Nia," she adds, pointing to the woman who is shorter like my mom. Nia is holding a little girl in her arms who has lots of small black braids in her hair that swing back and forth when she turns her head.

"My hair would look good in braids," Dragon says. I don't point out that he doesn't have any hair.

These neighbors are a lot different from our old neighbor Ms. Reilly. Ms. Reilly was an older white woman who didn't have any kids, didn't smile a lot, and gave out raisins on Halloween. These new neighbors are a black family with two moms and three kids, and they seem to like smiling. I'm hoping they give out candy on Halloween.

"This is our oldest son, Jayden," Nia says,

reaching up to put her hand on Jayden's shoulder. He's the tallest of everyone here, except for my dad. Jayden looks older. Like high school old. "Here's Addie," Nia says about the girl in her arms. "And this is Michael. He's starting first grade. We're lucky. The elementary school is only a couple of blocks away," she says, and points down the street.

"Mom, I gotta go meet the guys," Jayden says. He waves to us and takes off.

"Teenagers never stay around for long." Paula sighs.

"I'm looking forward to that," Dad says, before Mom pokes him in the arm.

I look at Michael. He keeps looking at me and Dragon from behind his glasses and then looking away.

"It's nice to meet you all," Mom says, and introduces us. She tells Michael that Ellie and I are starting second grade. He quickly looks at us again.

"Michael's not usually so quiet," Paula says, and laughs. "You should come to our Labor Day weekend barbecue on Monday," she tells us. "Our neighbors are always welcome. We'll have hamburgers, grilled chicken . . ."

"I'm not hearing marshmallows," Dragon says, unimpressed.

"Corn on the cob, fruit salad . . ."

"We can bring a pasta dish!" Mom says.

"Wonderful!" Nia says.

"I'm still not hearing marshmallows," Dragon huffs.

"And we'll have pies, of course," Paula adds.

"Oh, pies!" Dragon says happily.

"Warren loves pie," Dad says, tousling my hair.

Addie points at me suddenly. "Warri," Addie says, and swings her braids back and forth. "Warri."

Oh no. "Warren," I say. "War-ren."

"Warri-Boo."

Ellie and Michael giggle.

"Looks like you made your first friend," Ellie whispers to me.

"She doesn't count!" I say.

"Warri."

I take Dragon and run into the house. I look back and see that Dad is talking to the moving guys and Mom and Ellie are still talking with Paula and Nia. Addie waves at me. I stick out my tongue at her.

"She was cute," Dragon says.

"She called me 'Warri-Boo.'"

"I wonder if she likes marshmallows."

"I don't know but I bet she doesn't like jousting," I say.

"What's jousting?" a voice behind me says.

I turn around and see Michael there.

"A long sword game only really talented and professional kids and dragons can play," I say.

"I used to play in this house all the time," Michael says, and bounces around the room. "My best friend Jake lived here before they moved. You're probably going to have his room. Want me to show you his room? It faces the backyard. They had a trampoline but they took it when they moved. I really miss it. His dad always made pancakes on weekends. Does your dad make pancakes? Do you always carry that dragon with you? Want me to show you Jake's room? I mean, your room?"

I remember Michael giggled when Addie called me "Warri-Boo."

"I can find it," I say.

Michael looks disappointed. He opens his mouth like he's about say another thousand things, but then just shrugs and leaves.

Ellie comes marching in soon after with a big smile.

"Three girls walked by after you left. They're in second grade, too. I now have three new friends. And you only have one."

"She doesn't count! I don't have any new friends yet!" I say. Ellie is still beaming.

Dragon shakes his head at me. He looks a lot like Mom when he does that.

4

Pie Contest

Saturday and Sunday are supposed to be spent unpacking. I make sure I unpack all the important stuff like my comic book collection and Dragon's wing covers for when he gets chilly at night. When my mom notices that I've been wearing the same clothes since Friday, she tells me to keep unpacking and find something new to wear.

I try to unpack more, but there are too many important things to get done first. I have to figure out how loudly I can bang on the floor of my room until Ellie can hear it and it annoys her. Then Dragon has to see how fast he can go down the banister on my skateboard. He keeps trying until he breaks the record from our last house. And finally we have to spend time finding new hiding places for marshmallows.

At dinnertime Sunday, Dad puts his hand on my shoulder and tells me that if I don't unpack enough clothes to wear something new to the barbecue on Monday, I can't go. I don't think missing the barbecue is a big loss but Dragon insists we check it out.

"This is a perfect opportunity to make new friends," he says on Monday afternoon as I reach into a box and pull some clothes out. "Plus, there could be jousting, pie-eating contests, flaming ring tosses, flaming bubbles, and pie-eating contests."

"I don't think it's that kind of barbecue," I tell him after I stuff the clothes into a dresser drawer.

"Maybe not yet, but it *could* be," he replies, and twiddles his claws together.

"What are you planning?" I ask.

"You mean what am I *not* planning?" he says, and raises his eyebrows a few times.

"You're going to get me in trouble, aren't you? Maybe you should stay inside," I suggest, but Dragon is already running past me down the stairs.

Downstairs I find Dragon, my parents, and Ellie waiting in the kitchen. Mom is putting a cover on the pasta dish.

"Ready to go over?" she asks.

"Am I ever!" Dragon says, beaming.

I try to grab Dragon, but he wiggles past my dad and out the back door to the backyard.

There are already a lot of people in Michael's backyard. His moms are grilling food on their deck. Jayden is talking with a bunch of older girls while bouncing Addie on his knees. Addie is playing with a bubble wand, and Michael is nearby pouring chips into a bowl at the food table. I don't know any of the other people.

My parents go to talk with other adults and Ellie runs to join a badminton game, but I don't see where Dragon went to.

"Hi, Warren!" Michael calls to me, and I walk over. "Want some chips? We have plain, ranch, cheddar, the super spicy kind . . . Hey, who ate half the bowl of spicy chips already?"

I follow the trail of chip crumbs from the table over to where Addie is sitting on Jayden's lap. Dragon is stuffing the last bit of spicy chips into his mouth while watching Addie blow bubbles. He gives a loud burp and blows a small blast of fire onto a huge bubble that comes from Addie's bubble wand.

"Bubble!" Addie wails, and starts to cry. Jayden looks at her in confusion.

"Did that bubble catch on fire?" Michael asks. He rubs his eyes like he can't believe what just happened.

"Wasn't it great?" Dragon says proudly. "Why have boring, non-flaming bubbles when you can have exciting, flaming bubbles?"

"Maybe it was too close to the grill," I say, and grab Dragon by the neck.

I start to walk away with Dragon when I realize Michael is right beside us.

"Where'd your dragon come from?" he asks. "I didn't even see him there before. He looks like a fun toy. My mom said I used to carry a stuffed owl doll with me everywhere but I don't remember and it's Addie's now anyway. She takes all my old toys. I wish I had a twin instead. Do you like being a twin or would you rather have an older brother or a younger sister? Or an older sister or a younger brother?"

"He talks more than I do," Dragon says, clearly impressed.

"I guess it's okay being a twin," I say.

Ellie suddenly runs up to us. "Hi, Michael," she says nicely, and then turns to me. "I made *four* new friends." She smiles triumphantly and walks away.

"And sometimes it's not okay being a twin," I add.

"Maybe it'd be better to not have any brothers or sisters and just live with a dragon doll," Michael says, and laughs.

I know he didn't mean any harm by it but Dragon begins to huff and puff.

"Did he just call me a doll? Seriously?" Dragon jumps out of my hands and marches away.

"Sometimes I think it'd be better to not have siblings *or* dragons," I reply.

"They're bringing out the pies!" Michael exclaims, and points to the food table. "We gotta hurry and get a piece of the chocolate cream pie. It's the best one! My aunt Rose puts little marshmallows all over the top."

We start to walk over when Jayden stops us. "Mom says you have to help bring out some more plates and napkins and stuff," he says to Michael.

"Argh," Michael says. "Fine, but I'll be

right back!" he tells me, and rushes off.

I go check out the pie table, looking for the chocolate cream pie Michael mentioned. I notice a familiar set of pointy ears poking out from behind a blueberry pie before they quickly disappear.

"Dragon!" I try to whisper under the table. "Dragon, stay away from the pies!"

"Mm . . . pie . . . mm . . ." I hear. I look under the tablecloth and see that Dragon has eaten almost an entire chocolate cream pie. He gives me a very happy, sleepy smile before he tips over onto the ground and starts to snore.

I grab the pie dish. I try to think of where to put it without anyone noticing, but when I turn around, Nia and Michael are standing in front of me holding napkins and paper plates.

"Well, a growing boy has to eat what he has to eat," Nia says, and laughs.

"You finished it *all*?" Michael says. "In, like, one minute???"

"Warren, did you eat that whole pie?" Mom
asks, walking over with Dad right behind her.

"Um, I gotta go do something. . . ." I say. I
put the pie dish on the food table and reach

under to grab Dragon. I try not to notice everyone staring at us as I walk back to our house.

I put Dragon on my bed. Since I don't have anything else to do, I work on unpacking the rest of my boxes.

When Dragon finally wakes up a couple of hours later, he rubs his eyes and yawns.

"That was a good barbecue," he says. "There was no jousting but I'm pretty sure I won the pie-eating contest. How many new friends did you make?"

"None," I tell him.

"Don't worry. You'll make lots at school tomorrow. Just don't do anything embarrassing like lose a pie-eating contest."

"I don't think it's that kind of school," I say.

"Maybe not yet, but it *could* be," he says, and then immediately falls back asleep.

5

First Impressions

At breakfast the next morning, I'm too anxious to eat much. Just one piece of toast with cream cheese and jelly, two bowls of Monster Marshmallow Madness cereal, and three cups of orange juice. Dragon is still sleeping in bed when I come in to grab my backpack.

"I'm leaving for school," I say as I shove in some pencils.

"You know I have to get my beauty sleep," Dragon says, and yawns. I toss him a couple of Monster Madness Marshmallows that I sneaked from breakfast. He roasts them a little with fire from his snout before eating them in one gulp.

"Come on, Warren and Ellie!" I hear my dad call.

I pull on my baseball cap, take my backpack, and run to the stairs to see that Ellie is already at the door with our dad. Our mom left after breakfast to start her new job. Dad works as a graphic designer from our home in his office room. That means he's able to take us to school and pick us up, but after school Ellie and I are supposed to pretend to get along so he can get work done. We usually forget to pretend.

"Wait for me!" Dragon shouts, and jumps into my backpack. I don't have time to argue with Dragon about staying home. I push him down as best I can so Dad doesn't see him. He doesn't like it when I bring Dragon to school with me in case I might lose him.

"Excited for school?" Dad asks. "I know it's only a few blocks away, but I'm still walking with you. . . ."

Ellie and I burst out the door as soon as Dad opens it.

"Wait for me!" he yells, but we're already past our driveway.

Ellie stops suddenly and turns to me.

"Look, I know I'm going to make more friends than you, but you're my brother and I don't always hate-hate you so I just want to say . . . don't be weird, okay?"

"What? I'm not weird," I say.

Ellie rolls her eyes and walks away.

"I'm not weird, right?" I ask.

"It's scary how *not* weird you are," Dragon calls out.

"I *know*," I say.

✖ ✖ ✖

Dad catches up with me and Ellie and we soon see two girls walking with their mom. Ellie walks over to them and begins talking with the girls while Dad and the mom introduce themselves.

I look around and see a boy with a baseball cap. His arms are crossed and he's walking a few paces away from his mom.

Dragon has climbed to the top of my backpack and moved the zipper open a bit to peek his head out. "Try and be his friend!" he says, and points to the kid with the baseball cap.

"Okay. Wait, how do I make a friend again?" I ask.

"Impress him with something you have that

he doesn't have. He'll want to be your friend real quick," Dragon says.

I slow my pace until I'm walking near the boy.

"Hi," I say.

He scowls at me.

"Mom, I don't want to start school today!" he says. His mom ignores him.

"What's wrong with school today?" I ask.

"My grandpa is visiting and I want to stay home with him," the boy says.

"When my grandpa visits I always get to stay home with him," I say. I do not say I made that up.

"My grandpa always gives me ice cream at breakfast, buys me ten new video games, and takes me to see whatever movie I want," the boy says.

"Well, my grandpa . . . reads to me," I say. The boy scowls. I do not think he is impressed.

Ellie runs over to me. "Two new friends," she says, beaming.

The boy and his mom walk ahead of us.

"I made a new friend too," I tell her. I do not say I do not even want to be friends with this boy.

"Really? What's your new friend's name?" Ellie asks. She looks like she might not believe me.

"Uh. . . ."

"Grandpa," Dragon says.

"Grandpa," I say.

"What?"

"It's his nickname!"

Ellie shakes her head.

The school bell rings and Dad hurries us to the schoolyard where he finds the teacher signs for our classroom lines before saying good-bye. Ellie is with a Mr. Whittle and I have a Mrs. Tierney. Ellie is already talking with kids in her line.

I look around and see the baseball cap boy in my classroom line. He sees me and scowls again, but I notice he is not talking with anyone.

All the other kids must know each other from being in school together last year and are talking and playing.

I hear my name being called.

"Warren! Hey, Warren!"

I look around and see Michael in one of the first grade lines. He is waving to me.

I give a small wave back.

"You're friends with a first grader?" the boy in the baseball cap says, and snickers.

"He's just my neighbor," I say. I do not say I would rather be in Michael's line.

Mrs. Tierney comes out and introduces herself to all of the students in our line. She reminds me of my teacher in my old town. Nice but very tired even though it's still the morning.

"Warren and Nicky, you both need to remove your caps," Mrs. Tierney says before walking to the front of the line. Nicky removes his cap and scowls at me like it's my fault he has to take it off. I scowl back and put my cap in my backpack. At least I know his name now.

"I can tell she doesn't joust," Dragon whispers to me, and I agree with him.

After the school bell rings, all of the kids in our class follow Mrs. Tierney into the school and to our classroom. When we arrive, Mrs. Tierney asks us to sit where our names are on pieces of paper at desks throughout the classroom. Luckily my seat isn't next to Nicky but next to a girl with curly hair who gives a little smile when I sit.

"Here's your chance for another friend," Dragon says. "Give her a compliment."

I try to push Dragon back down into the backpack but he just sticks his head out again.

I turn to the girl. "Hi, I'm Warren. Uh, your hair is very curly," I say.

"Yeah, I know," she says, and rolls her eyes. "I'm Alison Cohen. There are three Alisons in our grade, but I'm the only one with red hair. You're lucky. You're the only Warren in our grade."

I don't say anything, because I never thought to feel lucky about my name before.

"Did you bring your dragon for show-and-tell?" Alison asks. "They just do that in kinder-garten."

"Oh, I didn't know," I say. I do not say I knew that from my last school. I push Dragon down again.

"More compliments!" Dragon says, muffled. "More! More!"

"Your eyes are as white as marshmallows.

And you do not smell like rotten pumpkins," I say.

Alison gives me a weird look.

"Everyone, Warren Nesbitt is the only student in our class new to the school," Mrs. Tierney says from the front of the classroom. "Can we please give him a warm welcome?"

"Welcome, Warren," the class says.

Alison scooches her chair away from me.

"That went well," Dragon says. "So when's lunch?"

6

Eating Lunch, Sharing Lunch

When Mrs. Tierney says it's time to line up for lunch I see Alison bring along her backpack.

"You can take your bag to lunch?" I ask.

"Sure," Alison says. "I have my art journal in it if I want to use it after lunch at recess." I see that some other kids are taking their backpacks as well.

I hoist my backpack with Dragon in it over my shoulder.

"I am *starving*," I hear him moan from inside. I think I even hear Dragon's stomach growling.

"Do they serve marshmallows in the cafeteria?" I ask.

Alison gives me that weird look again.

"They serve, like, lunch food," she says. "You can get cookies for dessert."

I hear Dragon snort in disappointment.

"I guess it'll be okay," I say.

Mrs. Tierney seems very happy we get to eat, as she smiles more than she has all morning when we arrive at the cafeteria.

"Have a good lunch! I'll see you after recess," she calls out, and quickly leaves.

Half the class brings their lunch bags to a long table and the other half lines up to buy food.

I get in the food line and pile a milk carton, grilled cheese sandwich, bag of cookies, grapes, and a soft pretzel with mustard onto my plate.

The only seat left at the table for my class is at the end across from Nicky. He's looking unhappy again, but this time I don't blame him.

His lunch includes a squashed tuna sandwich, a banana that looks more brown than yellow, and some odd-looking cracker.

I sit down and take a few pieces of the grilled cheese sandwich to give to Dragon.

"This is a great time to make new friends," Dragon says in between bites. "I know! You can share some of your delicious meal with the other kids. People like making friends with sharers."

I hold up the grilled cheese sandwich.

"Not the sandwich!" Dragon says. "No one shares sandwiches. Especially gooey, cheesy sandwiches that dragons need to keep up their strength."

I hold up the milk. Dragon shakes his head.

"What am I going to wash the sandwich down with?"

I hold up the pretzel.

"What am I going to eat as

my after-sandwich snack?"

I hold up the grapes.

"You can't share the grapes. I need them for my digestion."

I hold up the bag of cookies. Now Dragon just looks mad and reaches his arms out to grab the cookies. He stuffs the whole bag in his mouth and finishes it in one gulp.

"We can make friends later," he says, and burps.

"Are you saving those cookies for later?" Nicky asks. He must have seen me put them in my bag before Dragon scarfed them down.

"Uh, yeah," I say.

"This is my cookie for lunch," Nicky says, and holds up the odd-looking cracker.

"Sorry," I say.

Nicky shrugs and

takes a bite. "My grandpa will take me for ice cream after school."

"Would you like some pretzel?" I ask, ignoring Dragon's snorts from below.

Nicky eyes me warily.

"Okay ... sure," he says and takes half of the pretzel.

I throw a couple of pieces of pretzel to Dragon and begin to eat the rest.

"Can I have more?" Nicky asks.

"I already gave you half," I say, and take another bite.

"I'll trade you my sandwich," Nicky offers.

I look at the mushy tuna sandwich.

"No thanks," I say. "I don't like tuna." I do not say I do like tuna but only when it's not in a mushy sandwich.

"You're not a good friend," Nicky says, and takes his lunch stuff away from the table.

I look around and see that most of the kids at the table have left to go outside for recess.

I give the rest of my food to Dragon. I don't feel hungry anymore. I had a chance to make a friend and I messed it up. Now instead of one hundred new friends I still have none.

"Am I a good friend?" I ask Dragon.

Dragon pats his belly and burps again. "I've never had any complaints," he says, and then falls asleep for a nap.

7

Dragon's Sporty Advice

I leave the top of my backpack open to give Dragon fresh air as he sleeps and walk outside for recess.

Kids are running all over, but I only recognize a few faces from Mrs. Tierney's class.

Alison is sitting under a tree with colored pencils and her journal. I see Ellie with a group of girls playing by the monkey bars.

I go over to a long bench and sit down, when I realize Michael is already there. He's looking at a bunch of boys playing soccer nearby on the grass.

"They won't let me play," he says to me. "They're all second and third graders and they said I have to wait a year. I'm really good, though. I bet I'm even better than they are if they gave me a chance to show them. Jayden plays with me sometimes, and he says I'm really good, and he's really, really good and plays on a real soccer team and everything so I know it's true."

"Okay," I say. I do not know what else to say.

Michael looks over at me and then peers into my bag.

"Do you bring that dragon doll around everywhere?" he asks.

"Was I just called a doll?" Dragon says. I see that he's wide awake and starting to huff and puff. "Seriously?"

"Shh . . ." I whisper to him.

"I can't calm down! I was just called a doll by Michael. *Again*. I'm going to need five bags of marshmallows, extra-large and fluffy, to even think about calming down."

"Dragon isn't a doll," I say. "He's . . . a keepsake."

"What's that?" Michael asks.

"I keep him for the sake of annoying my sister," I explain. "I don't usually take him to school. I just forgot he was in my bag today."

"Oh," Michael says. "Do you like soccer?"

"Say yes! Say yes!" Dragon shouts. He's moved on from being called a doll.

"Yes," I say. I do not say the soccer I play involves Dragon and me hitting a soccer ball into mud piles to see how much mud we can splash around and get on my clothes.

"Great!" Michael says with a smile. "We can ask for a ball from the recess lady over there."

Michael begins to stand up but stops when Ewan and Darryl, two of the second graders I know from Mrs. Tierney's class, come over. I can see they had been playing soccer with the other guys.

"Henry tripped and hurt his knee. He went to the nurse, so we need another player," Ewan says to me. "Do you want his spot?"

I look at the group of soccer players waiting for me and stand up to join them. There must be fifteen or twenty kids there. If I play well enough they would probably become my friends. I think. If I play with Michael, he would be just one friend. Plus, I can always play with him after school since we're neighbors. I turn to ask

Michael if he wants to play later, but he's already gone.

I look over at Ellie, who is now playing basketball with even more girls. I have to catch up with all the friends she's making.

"Sure," I say, and stand up.

"Don't get nervous," I hear Dragon shout from my bag. He says this because he knows I am nervous. "Regular soccer is super easy. Just kick the ball in the goal!"

I nod my head and walk over to the soccer group. Darryl gives me a quick rundown of the game, which I should be listening to, but I keep my eyes on the ball and the two goals.

"Okay, break!" one of the kids says, and everyone moves around to different positions. I move two steps back. No one says anything so I think I'm in the right place.

Kids start kicking the ball around and it's nowhere near me. I move toward the goal and hope the ball comes closer so I can kick it in.

Darryl has the ball and three kids are running at him. He looks around and sees me behind him. He kicks the ball to me and I can't believe how easy this will be. No one is around me at all. I turn toward the goal and kick it in.

I pump my fists in the air, but for some reason I hear groans instead of whooping.

"Why did you score for the other team?!?" Ewan shouts at me.

All of the kids on our team are looking at me and seem upset. The kids on the other team are snickering.

"Oh, so you're playing *that* kind of soccer," I say.

"What other kind of soccer is there?" Ewan demands.

"The kind of soccer kids at my old school played," I say. I do not say kids at my old school probably played normal soccer, too. "It might be too advanced for most players."

Ewan opens his mouth like he wants to say something but can't think of what to say.

Darryl looks like he's trying not to laugh.

I'm leaving to get my bag when Ellie suddenly runs up to me. "Six more friends just at recess!" she says, starting to count on her fingers before stopping. "There's too many to count right now."

I shrug as though I don't care.

"How many friends have you made?" she asks.

"It's about quantity, not quality," I tell her, remembering what our dad said on Christmas morning.

"You mean quality, not quantity?" Ellie asks.

"Yes," I say. I do not say I do not know because I'm not really sure what our dad was saying to begin with.

Ellie sighs. The bell rings and she turns to run inside the school.

"This day is the worst," I say. Dragon doesn't respond. He's probably upset he gave me such horrible advice about kicking the ball into the goal without telling me to first make sure it was the right goal.

"At least Mom promised marshmallows for

snack after school," I add to make Dragon feel better, but he still doesn't answer. Everyone is running to get inside the school, so I hoist my bag over my shoulder and run in with them. Dragon will be happy once we get home and eat and play our own games. After all, this day can't get any worse.

8

Lost

It got worse.

Because at the end of school, just as I am looking forward to going home, I look into my bag and see that Dragon . . . is *gone*! As in, he is not there, in my bag, where he's supposed to be. He's not sleeping or eating or jousting or anything in my bag. Because he's not in my bag!!!!

Mrs. Tierney is telling everyone to line up.

I consider my options. I could throw a tantrum so bad that Mrs. Tierney would have to leave to get the principal to help, which would give me time to look around the classroom for Dragon. But then I'd be known as the kid who threw tantrums in addition to being the kid who kicked the soccer ball into the wrong goal.

I could pretend to be sick and throw up so Mrs. Tierney would have to get the nurse and the janitor, which would give me time to look for Dragon. But then I'd be known as the kid who threw up.

"Dragon . . ." I whisper as I walk over to the line, bending to look under the desks. "Dragon . . ."

"What are you doing?" Alison asks. She's given me the weird look so many times that it doesn't look so weird anymore.

"Nothing," I say.

"Were you looking for your homework sheet?" Darryl asks, and holds up a piece of paper.

"Thanks," I say, and take the sheet. I do not

say I was not looking for my homework sheet and would have been okay losing it instead of Dragon.

"I was new last year," Darryl says. "The first day is always the worst."

I do not know what to say so I just nod my head.

Before I know it we're walking out of the classroom and toward the front doors of the school.

All I can think about is poor Dragon. He probably got hungry for an after-lunch snack and went looking for one. He could be in the cafeteria or another kid's lunchbox or trapped on top of a cubby.

"Warren! Over here!" I see my dad waving to me from the pick-up line with Ellie by his side. "How was your day?" he asks.

"It was okay," I say. I do not say it was not okay and was really the most stinky, stupid, and terrible day ever.

"Dad, I invited some friends over for this afternoon," Ellie says.

"Ellie, I have a lot of work to do in the home office today," Dad says.

"You wanted me to make new friends," Ellie points out.

"All right, but just for today." Dad sighs and turns to me. "Did you make any new friends today, Warren?"

I scuff my shoe on the pavement as we walk.

I think about Nicky. We were friends for a minute at lunch, but I don't want to give him all my food every day just to be friends. I think about Alison. Lots of weird looks doesn't seem to add up to a friendship, even though she's nice. I think about Ewan and Darryl and all the boys playing soccer. Darryl turned out to be pretty okay, but I don't know how much I have in common with him.

I think about Dragon. He was my one best friend, and now I don't even know where he is.

I don't answer, and Dad doesn't ask me again.

When we get home I run into the kitchen and put out marshmallows on a plate, in hopes that Dragon will smell them and find his way back.

"You're going to eat all those?" Ellie asks as she reaches for a box of crackers.

"No, they're for Dragon," I say.

"Where is he?" she says, and takes out grapes from the fridge.

"I'm not sure. I might have . . . lost him."

Ellie gasps. "You lost your one and only friend?"

"Yes! I lost my one and only friend, okay?" I know I look crazy with my hands waving everywhere but I don't care. "You win. Once again, you are right about everything. I did not make a hundred new friends. I didn't even make one new friend and I don't want to make any friends at school anyway. They don't know it's totally okay to kick the soccer

ball into any goal because the whole point of a
soccer ball is to throw it into mud puddles and
no one understands compliments and it's not
my fault when kids have yucky lunches and I
don't want to share all my lunch because I get
hungry, too."

"We need cookies for this," Ellie declares, and goes on her tippy toes to get the hidden stash of cookies it took us the whole weekend to find in the new house.

Ellie hands me a couple of cookies and we eat for a bit.

"You have to tell Dad," she says.

"I can't," I say. "Dad told me not to bring him to school and I did, and now he'll get mad if he finds out."

We both look toward the office room where Dad is working.

"Okay, we gotta figure this out then," Ellie says. "Where did you last see Dragon?"

"He was with me at lunch. And he was in my bag at recess."

"How about after recess?"

"I didn't see him after recess."

"So he got lost at recess?" Ellie asks.

"I don't know," I say, and think some more. "I had him when I sat on the bench and talked to Michael. . . . Hey!"

"What?"

"Michael saw Dragon. Maybe he knows."

"Let's go ask him," Ellie suggests.

"Dad, we're going to our neighbors'! Be right back!" we shout at the office door, and leave before Dad can say no.

9

Found

We run to Michael's house and I ring the door-
bell. His mom Paula opens the door and looks
surprised but happy to see us. Addie is in her
arms and points at me.

"Warri-Boo," she coos. I ignore her.

"Is Michael home?" Ellie asks.

"Yes, he's up in his room. I can go get him. . . ."

"It's okay. We'll go to him!" Ellie says, and we
run past Paula and Addie up the stairs. We don't
know where Michael's room is, but when I see a
door with pictures of soccer players taped to it, I
go over and knock.

"Who's knocking?" I hear Michael ask. I
open the door.

Michael is on the floor of his room setting up action figures and stuffed animals in between two mini soccer goals. And right there, in the very middle, with a soccer ball by his foot, is Dragon.

"Uh . . . want to play?" Michael asks.

"That's my brother's doll!" Ellie shouts.

"Did she just call me a doll?" Dragon asks. He jumps up and walks slowly over to me, taking care to avoid all the actual dolls and sports toys on Michael's floor. "Took you long enough to find me," he says, and lets out a big huff.

"He's not a doll," Michael says. "He's a dragon."

I'm about to agree with Michael, but then I remember he stole Dragon.

"Why'd you steal Dragon?" I ask.

Michael looks down at his floor. "I'm sorry," he says. "I didn't mean to steal him. I just wanted to play at recess, and you got up to play with all the second and third graders instead. And then I saw your dragon in your bag and remembered how you always have him with you, so I thought he'd be fun to play with and then I forgot to put him back in your bag."

"You forgot?" Ellie asks.

Michael scratches his head like he's trying to think real hard. "Maybe I didn't forget. He's really fun to play with, so I on purpose didn't remember. I'm really sorry. Please don't tell my mom. Or wait to tell my mom Nia because she never remembers to punish me."

Michael's mom Paula shows up at the door. "I talked to your dad," she says to me and Ellie. "He says you can play here or Michael can play at your house but Ellie needs to come home for when her friends arrive."

Michael looks at us with lots of worry on his face. I'm glad he's worried, but I don't want to get him in trouble, because I'm always in trouble and I know it doesn't feel good.

"It's okay," I say. "We're both going home now."

"Thanks," Michael whispers as we go.

10

Chocolate-Covered Bananas

Ellie's friends are already starting to arrive when we get back, so she leaves me to greet them. I take Dragon to the kitchen, and he immediately scarfs down most of the marshmallows.

"I can't believe you let yourself be dragon-napped," I say. "I was really worried."

"It's not my fault," Dragon says, and burns a marshmallow to a crisp before inhaling it. "I didn't have my bodyguards with me."

"But if Michael took you right next door, why didn't you just walk home?" I ask.

"He kept wanting to play," Dragon says. "I was waiting for my chance to escape when you rescued me."

"Was it horrible?"

Dragon thinks for a minute. "No, it wasn't horrible. I missed you, but Michael's pretty fun.

He recognizes my superior athletic skill and made me the soccer captain, the basketball captain, and the ice hockey captain. He also has great snacks. No marshmallows, but he did have chocolate-covered bananas."

"I like chocolate-covered bananas," I say.

"They're really yummy." Dragon finishes the marshmallows and hops down to the floor. "Can we play at Michael's now? He said he's going to show me his tree house, and I bet he'd invite you, too."

"I'm not friends with Michael!" I say. "He stole you! From me!"

"He said he's sorry," Dragon says.

I stomp around the kitchen to show how upset I still am.

"Did I mention he's got a tree house?" Dragon asks.

"I like tree houses," I say.

"And you like chocolate-covered bananas," Dragon adds.

"That's true," I agree. "It's kinda like, we have stuff in common."

"Friends have stuff in common," Dragon says.

Dragon follows me out of the kitchen. We find Dad picking up shoes and jackets from the hallway where Ellie's friends left them.

"Dad, can I go see Michael again?" I ask.

"That means you'll be out of the house? Yes," he says, and waves me off.

Dragon and I run next door. Michael and Addie are playing with colored chalk in their driveway, while Paula talks on the phone nearby. Michael looks up at me.

"Do you like marshmallows?" I ask him.

"Sure," he says.

"Do you like playing games like soccer but with other rules that don't include goals?"

"I guess so," Michael answers. "But I like regular soccer, too."

"Friends compromise," Dragon whispers to me.

' "I can like regular soccer," I say. "I just have to learn a little more about it."

"Jayden said he'll give me a lesson tomorrow after school," Michael says. "He'll teach you, too, if you want."

"Okay," I say, and nod my head. "So?"

"So what?"

"So Warri-Boo," Addie says, and giggles.

"She's so cute," Dragon says.

"So do you want to be friends?" I ask.

"Oh. Yeah!" Michael says, and smiles.

"Okay, I'll be right back," I tell him, and run back into my house with Dragon.

I find Ellie in the family room with her friends.

"Psst!" I say to Ellie, but everyone ends up looking at me. "I need my sister," I say, and pull Ellie to the hallway.

"What is it?" she asks.

"Two," I say, and hold up two fingers.

"Two what?"

"I have two friends."

Ellie smiles. "You mean three."

"Addie doesn't count!"

Ellie rolls her eyes. "I mean me, you loony."

"Oh," I say. I smile. Ellie's right. Sometimes we are friends.

"Wait right here!" Dad says suddenly from behind me. "Keep smiling! Let me get my phone so I can get a picture for Mom."

"For the record, I did make sixty-four friends so far," Ellie says.

And sometimes Ellie is wrong and we aren't friends.

"Yeah, but most of them smell like rotten cabbage," I say.

"Dad!"

"Okay, okay," I say. "Some of them smell like rotten boogies."

"So close," Dad says with his phone in hand.

"I'm going over to Michael's," I tell them, and quickly get out of there.

"You know, you basically have one hundred

friends," Dragon says to me as we walk back to Michael's house.

"How's that?"

"I'm worth at least ninety-eight friends. I'm extraordinarily fun, sporty, agile, handsome, adorable, and fierce. And modest, too."

"With Michael and Ellie that makes one hundred!" I exclaim. Turns out I was listening during some math lessons at school.

"We should celebrate with marshmallows," he says.

"And chocolate-covered bananas," I add.

"Marshmallows melted onto chocolate-covered bananas," Dragon suggests.

"That's a little weird," I say.

"It's not weird. It's perfect," Dragons replies.

I think about it for a minute. He's right.

Turn the page to
read a chapter of

WARREN
& Dragon
Weekend with Chewy

WARREN & Dragon

Weekend with Chewy

by Ariel Bernstein

Illustrated by Mike Malbrough

Everyone Loves Chewy

My dad is waiting for me outside the school in the pick-up area. Mrs. Tierney walks over to him and motions to Chewy before giving Dad a bag of hamster food. Dad smiles like he's not sure if he's really happy. It's the same smile he gave me when I made him a necktie out of marshmallows I glued together for his birthday.

"I look forward to your report," Mrs. Tierney says to me before going back into the school. I do not say I am also looking forward to it because I don't know what report she is talking about. But now I have to write some sort of report over the weekend, too. This is just great. Maybe I can bribe Dragon with marshmallows to write one for me.

My twin sister Ellie's class lets out, and she walks over to us.

"Oh, what a cute little hamster!" Ellie squeals, and looks into the cage.

"He looks kind of ugly to me," I say.

"He's adorable," Ellie insists. "And he doesn't talk back either," she adds, looking at me.

"What's wrong with talking back?" I say. I like it when Dragon talks back to me. He says really good stuff most of the time.

"Dad, can we have a pet for real?" Ellie asks. "Not a dragon toy," she adds, shooting me a look like I was going to interrupt.

She's right, I was going to interrupt. I was going to say I don't want any new pets. Dragon is enough of a handful. Plus, he's not a toy. He's a real dragon pet, and it's not my fault no one else knows it.

"Pets are a lot of responsibility," Dad says. "You have to take care of them and feed them and make sure they don't get hurt. . . ."

"I can do all that!" Ellie pleads.

"Ellie, you hardly ever get through a whole week with the chores you already have," Dad says.

"Ellie has chores?" I ask.

"So do you!" Ellie says.

"I have chores?" I ask. "Wait, is this why I haven't gotten my allowance in forever?"

Dad looks at me and shakes his head.

Ellie glances over at me like she's thinking about something. "What if I *prove* I can be responsible?" she asks Dad.

"You can start by making your bed every morning," Dad says.

Ellie doesn't reply but walks over to me.

"Are you okay, Warren?" Ellie asks me. She

is looking at Dad as though she wants Dad to hear her.

"Yes," I say. I do not say I can't figure out why Ellie is suddenly being so nice.

"Do you need to stop and rest? Are you thirsty?" Ellie asks, and pats my head.

"No," I say, ducking her hand.

"Watch out for that puddle!" Ellie shouts, and tries to grab my arm. I move backward and start to trip before I accidentally let go of the cage.

I land hard on the ground and Chewy's cage lands on my stomach. He runs around for a moment before taking a sip of water from the attached water dispenser.

"Warren!" Dad says. "Are you okay? What happened?"

"I'm okay," I mumble while getting up.

"Are you sure, Warren?" Ellie asks. "He needs so much care and attention," she says to Dad. "Don't worry, I'll watch out for him. Just like I'd do with a real pet."

Before I can tell Ellie to stay away, Michael

walks over with one of his moms, Paula, and Addie. Michael is in first grade and I'm in second, but we still hang out at recess and after school a lot. I guess you could say he's my best human friend. Dragon is my best dragon friend, although there's not much competition.

"What's that?" Michael asks, pointing at the cage.

"A hamster," I reply.

"You get to have a dragon *and* a hamster?" Michael says in awe. Like other people, Michael isn't able to hear Dragon talk. But unlike other people, Michael still gets how awesome Dragon is.

"All I ever had was a goldfish last year," Michael adds. "He lived a good life for a couple of weeks but then I overfed him and, well, you know."

I nod in understanding. I overfeed Dragon all the time, but luckily dragons don't die because of too much food.

"We only have the hamster for the weekend," Dad quickly points out.

"Hamster boo," Addie says, and giggles as she waves to Chewy in his cage.

I do not know why everyone likes Chewy so much. All he does is run on his wheel and eat his food.

When we get to our houses, Michael tells me he's going to start thinking of ideas to build our ramp tomorrow. I say I will, too, because building a ramp to trade snacks after bedtime is way more important than taking care of a hamster or writing a report. Luckily, I have a plan.